I0869415

World of Art

Exploring GRAPHIC ART

W.L. Kitts

ReferencePoint Press®

San Diego, CA

ReferencePoint Press®

Printed in the United States

For more information, contact:
ReferencePoint Press, Inc.
PO Box 27779
San Diego, CA 92198
www.ReferencePointPress.com

LIBRARY OF CONGRESS CATALOGING-IN-PUBLICATION DATA

Names: Kitts, W. L., author.
Title: Exploring graphic art / by W.L. Kitts.
Description: San Diego, CA : ReferencePoint Press, Inc., 2025. | Series: World of art | Includes bibliographical references and index.
Identifiers: LCCN 2024007376 (print) | LCCN 2024007377 (ebook) | ISBN 9781678208622 (library binding) | ISBN 9781678208639 (ebook)
Subjects: LCSH: Graphic arts. | Communication in art.
Classification: LCC NC997 .K475 2025 (print) | LCC NC997 (ebook) | DDC 744--dc23/eng/20240403
LC record available at https://lccn.loc.gov/2024007376
LC ebook record available at https://lccn.loc.gov/2024007377

Contents

Worth a Thousand Words

Art, in general, has historically been used to decorate, communicate, or share information. And human beings have been communicating and telling stories through images for tens of thousands of years. In fact, visual storytelling predates language. Prehistoric cave drawings are as much graphic art as Michelangelo's frescoes on the ceiling of the Vatican's Sistine Chapel; Andy Warhol's infamous 1962 *Campbell's Soup Cans* paintings; Banksy's self-destructing *Girl with Balloon* art installment; Carolyn Davidson's "swoosh" logo inspired by the angelic wings of Nike, the Greek goddess of victory; or Shepard Fairey's iconic *Hope* poster featuring then presidential hopeful Barack Obama. But it was in those caves approximately sixty-five thousand years ago that visual representations were presumably first used to communicate.

And although ancient drawings may not have a direct influence on modern-day art and design, they provide context for how visual communication has evolved over the centuries. Clearly, humans had a head start processing images over language. And it has been determined that the human brain processes images much faster than words. In fact, neuroscientists at the Massachusetts Institute of Technology found that individuals can identify images in as little as thirteen milliseconds—a mere fraction of the time it takes to blink. So maybe a picture really is worth a thousand words.

Exploring Graphic Art

Graphic art is a category of fine arts. Its goal is to persuade, entertain, or convey ideas, emotions, and information by using images and sometimes color and text. Graphic art is everywhere. It is a poster on a bedroom wall, a magazine on a nightstand, a cereal box at breakfast, and even graffiti in a schoolyard.

Graphic art is a broad term, though it is primarily reserved for 2-D art processes and visual artistic expressions, such as drawing, painting, photography, illustrating, calligraphy, etching, printmaking, and graphic design. Textural elements are also important in graphic art and usually reflect the choice of the medium and the surface—whether paper, canvas, stone, or wall (including cave walls)—that are used as the foundation for the artwork. All elements work in harmony to play a role in the creation of the visual image and in the idea being communicated.

> **WORDS IN CONTEXT**
>
> **medium: Material used in the creation of art, such as paint or ink**

And though not always necessary, graphic art sometimes includes text. Typography can be used to help communicate or highlight a visual story and can play a significant role in graphic design.

The Art of Graphic Design

The terms *graphic art* and *graphic design* are often used interchangeably. However, graphic design is a category of graphic art. In fact, graphic designers often combine other forms of graphic art, such as paintings, illustrations, and photography—as well as typography—in their designs.

> **WORDS IN CONTEXT**
>
> **typography: The arrangement of type by manipulating spacing and fonts to make it readable and visually appealing**

Graphic design is a form of visual communication that has generally been linked to advertising, whether branding a place, a product, or the

Girl with Balloon, *a mural by the anonymous British street artist known as Banksy, is a modern-day form of visual storytelling or graphic art. Visual storytelling has been a feature of human societies through the ages.*

artist. Graphic designers mostly work in marketing and create websites, packaging, and advertisements for everything from books to fashion to fast-food restaurants.

Modern-Day Design

For centuries, graphic designers used traditional tools to create their designs. However, in modern times pencils, inks, paints, and paper are being supplanted by their virtual counterparts. Digital tools produce images or enhance scanned 2-D artwork in a fraction of the time it takes to create the same art by hand.

Graphic designers also use digital tools to include 3-D elements and interactive features in their work to help attract and engage their target audience. For example, the Google home page logo often contains 3-D elements such as animations, slideshows, videos, and games. These Google Doodles—over five thousand since 1998—usually commemorate a holiday, world event, or person in history.

Digital tools have also pushed graphic designers to work almost exclusively online. And they are not just creating logos or ads. In the digital age graphic designers create websites, social media content, and virtual storefronts for a variety of digital devices. Designer Gargi Singh explains on LinkedIn, "One of the most notable changes in graphic design over the past decade has been the shift from print to digital. With the rise of social media and other digital platforms, designers are now creating content that is optimized for a wide range of digital devices, from desktop computers to smartphones and tablets."[1]

Evolving Art

Graphic art has come a long way since prehistoric cave drawings. Technology is rapidly changing how graphic artists create and do their jobs with just a click of a mouse. Paintbrushes and paint have been replaced by digital brushes and virtual paint. With all these technological advancements—including the role artificial intelligence (AI) now plays in design—graphic art is experiencing rapid and expansive growth.

Chapter One

The Evolution of Graphic Art

Art is almost as old as life. People have been telling stories visually since the dawn of civilization. Long before the Egyptians created hieroglyphics some five thousand years ago, early humans were communicating, expressing themselves, and sharing stories nonverbally on cave walls approximately sixty-five thousand years ago. "This is a solid 20,000 years before our modern human ancestors arrived in Europe," writer and graphic designer Hestie Barnard Gerber says. "Research confirms that the Paleolithic (Ice Age) cave paintings—which include paintings of mammals, as well as geometric designs and dots, were made by Europe's only inhabitants at the time—the Neanderthals."[2] Even if these are the first known instances of graphic art, occurring at a time when these human ancestors could not even speak, it is clear that the desire to create art has been a hallmark of all civilizations.

From Wood Blocks to Printing Presses

Humanity's need to share stories, express thoughts and emotions, and communicate has propelled the growth and spread of the arts. While drawing on cave walls or fashioning idols has been with humanity since its earliest history, the development of language and the inscribing of words onto clay tablets and then early forms of paper allowed for the preservation of and access to knowledge.

Many of the earliest earthen tablets, papyrus or wood scrolls, and bound paper books were supplemented with images to visually explain the text or simply decorate each unique work. One of the earliest ways in which images could be added to texts was through block printing. Historians can trace the block printing of images to China in the third century CE. However, mechanical block printing of texts did not emerge in China until the seventh century CE. Backward-written letters and images were carved into blocks of wood or clay, coated with a mixture of resin, ashes, and wax, and then pressed onto silk. Block printing of text on paper in China only dates to the eighth century CE. Both forms of block printing spread through Asia quickly.

The early methods of block printing were improved on in Korea in the mid-1200s. Instead of chiseling large blocks of wood, Choe Yun-ui, a minister seeking to print a fifty-volume Buddhist text, used

This Paleolithic-era painting of a horse head, discovered in a cave in France, is an example of how humans sought to express themselves and share stories thousands of years ago.

WORDS IN CONTEXT

movable type: A printing process in which individual letters or characters can be arranged and rearranged in various orders to produce documents

movable type, a process the Chinese had created using porcelain tile punches, as they were called, around 1040 CE. Choe Yun-ui cast his individual character punches in metal. The characters making up the book were inserted into a frame and then inked and printed multiple times. This printing technique could be set up and rearranged much more quickly than block carving.

In 1440 German inventor Johannes Gutenberg created a movable-type printing press in Europe, which helped speed book production in the West. The work of graphic artists could also be spread through books, handbills, posters, and other printed materials much faster since the images they created no longer needed to be individually hand drawn or painted. With these innovations, stories and images could travel more easily around the globe. As printing became faster and more affordable, there was an increased demand for books, newspapers, advertisements, and other printed materials—and thus, graphic artists.

Color Printing and the Power of Poster Art

By the 1800s chromolithography—the ability to print color—was introduced. This was another leap forward, particularly for advertising in the fashion world. Color provided more realism, and it allowed artists to use human models, in contrast to the cartoon-like sketches common at the time. In addition, nineteenth-century thinkers like Johann Wolfgang von Goethe produced theories that identified how colors could manipulate the emotions of viewers. The art of typography also progressed in the 1800s and 1900s. Fonts became as important an element in graphic art as color. And graphic artists and designers experimented with new styles as technology advanced.

In the 1900s the ability to mass print in color on mechanical printing presses led to an explosion of graphic art posters. Though

Illuminated Manuscripts

Illuminated manuscripts are handwritten books known for their elaborate hand-painted embellishments, primarily in silver and gold metal, to "illuminate" the text. Dating back to approximately 600 CE, these books feature ornate letters and tiny illustrations often in the margins of the manuscripts and were printed on the hides of animals such as cows and sheep. These ornamental books, which existed in many countries, were popular mostly in western European Christian culture and were often religious texts such as Bibles, prayer books, and choir books.

Most illuminated Christian texts were created by monks in monasteries in the eleventh century. The illustrations were added because, in the Middle Ages, many people—including some clergy—could not read. Having images helped make the texts accessible to those who might be familiar with the general story but could not understand the words—because of illiteracy or linguistic barriers. "By illuminating texts, skilled artists were able to beautify the pages of the Bible as a way to summarize, explain, and, ultimately, preserve its message," explains the not-for-profit ministry Crossway.

The demand for these works declined around 1600 after the invention of the printing press, the mass-production of books, and rising rates of public literacy.

Crossway, "A Brief Introduction to the History of the Illuminated Manuscript," Crossway, November 6, 2017. www.crossway.org.

often used for advertising purposes, these illustrated posters—essentially early-day memes—were also developed with slogans both to inform and educate populations.

During World War I, the US Committee on Public Information's Division of Pictorial Publicity recruited artists to design powerful graphics to support the war effort. For example, some were tasked with designing posters to encourage men to join the military; others, like famed New York painter and illustrator Norman Rockwell, contributed to the cause by painting posters to help sell war bonds. The Norman Rockwell Museum website explains:

WORDS IN CONTEXT

meme: An often humorous image or video that spreads virally on internet and social media sites

> During the First World War, illustrated posters inspiring public support served as a primary mechanism of mass communication. Imbued with iconic United States symbols like the

> Statue of Liberty, Uncle Sam, and the American flag, these posters were powerful reminders of the nation's engagement with four Liberty Loan campaigns, the War Savings Stamps program, the Victory Loan, and the American Red Cross.[3]

Graphic illustrations were also tapped as a source of social commentary. Empowering, memorable images were successfully used by the suffragettes to advocate for a woman's right to vote in the early 1900s. And during World War II, the US government used a poster campaign to attract women into the workforce while men were serving overseas. The iconic *Rosie the Riveter* poster was illustrated by J. Howard Miller and featured a strong, capable woman flexing her muscles, with the caption "We Can Do It!" According to the US Department of Labor website, "The campaign brought millions of women out of the home and into the workforce. To this day, Rosie the Riveter is still considered the most successful government advertising campaign in history."[4]

In the San Francisco music and art scene, posters were adorned with flowing, colorful imagery and an array of typefaces that ranged from Victorian script to puffy, cloudlike lettering. Such vibrant and dazzling prints were intended to reflect the psychedelic experience. In New York, Andy Warhol's experiments with pop art turned common objects and imagery into mass-produced art. His colorful prints of movie star Marilyn Monroe, for example, demonstrated how all images—whether iconic photos of celebrities, ever-present advertisements, or soup-can labels—were part of a popular culture that was marketed to the public. Like the rock posters, Warhol's art seemed to separate itself from fine art that people would have to visit in a museum. This new art resonated with young people, and it could be easily reproduced so that anyone could own a cheap copy.

Computer-Aided Art

Most of these early to mid-twentieth-century commercial arts were still created by artists using pencils, paints, inks, paper, and canvas. Graphic art in this respect was a labor-intensive process, and any corrections to a piece might result in an artist starting again from scratch. But all that changed with the advent of personal computing in the late 1970s and graphic design software created for public use. Computers allowed artists to use pixels—picture elements—to create art in a new medium. Photoshop, the world's best-known graphic design program, was first marketed in 1990 and gave computer artists the ability to erase mistakes, change colors, resize images, create typography, and rearrange elements in a design with just the click of a mouse.

This was especially valuable to graphic designers, who formerly had to painstakingly cut and paste their artwork—literally—using rulers, T-squares, and rubber cement every time a different font or color was requested from a boss or client. Consumer-based, user-friendly design software like Photoshop soon gave artists

The graphic design program Photoshop allows graphic artists and designers to erase mistakes, change colors, resize images, create typography, and rearrange elements in a design with just the click of a mouse.

more tools to customize, revise, and save their work. Working digitally with these tools allows artists and designers alike to create artwork much more efficiently and in less time. Even photographers can digitally adjust lighting, sharpness, and other aspects of a picture to produce better, clearer, and more pleasing photos. Harold Stark, a contributor to HuffPost, notes, "For the first time ever, something so robust and convenient had been made accessible to the general public. People flocked to it like sheep. While image manipulation remained an art for the selected few even a few years ago, this software made it possible for anyone to take up arms and become an expert in photography."[5]

In 1990, the same year Photoshop hit store shelves, the World Wide Web became accessible to everyone. "Graphic design evolved drastically over time, thanks to technology," blogger Rangan Das explains on the website of Artwork Flow, an AI marketing platform. "Easels and canvases have made way for computer screens and design tools in today's art—graphic design and technology always progressed together."[6] Having access to the internet has given artists a way to promote themselves, display their art, and reach a global audience.

The "Art" of Memes

It was not only artists who used the internet to reach audiences; clever creators began matching words with text to create memes. First spread in the 1990s on message boards, memes were often single-image posts that spread easily in social media culture. Some memes carry serious messages, but the majority are humorous or nonsensical. Some united movements like #MeToo and Black Lives Matter; others recycled pop culture images from movies or television and married them to parodic or ridiculous texts. Often, the more abstract the connection between words and image, the more pervasive the meme. Some creators drew their own mascots or took photos of their pets, and the internet turned them into icons.

Like poster art before them, memes were easy to post and share, but instead of being affixed to fences and walls in towns and cities, these internet "posters" went up across social media sites, reaching people and communities around the world within seconds. Memes became instantly recognizable and gave people a shared frame of reference. A recent article on the Mirage News website explains, "Internet memes carry a significant cultural weight, acting as a mirror to society. They echo collective experiences, concerns, and values, and reflect the zeitgeist of the digital age. Memes often emerge as responses to current events, popular culture, or social trends, and their popularity is determined by their relatability and the shareable value they offer."[7]

Some people question whether memes are art, just as they once questioned whether Warhol's pop art paintings of everyday objects such as Campbell's soup cans were art. Much like

Some people question whether memes are art, just as they once questioned whether Andy Warhol's pop art paintings of everyday objects such as Campbell's soup cans were art.

Memes: Graphic Art as Social Commentary

It has been proposed that memes—a visual language of today's generation—have their roots in the Dadaist anti-art movement. That movement, which is said to have inspired the art styles of surrealism and pop art, challenged both artistic and societal norms and was expressed through social and political commentary in reaction to World War I.

Today's memes are similar. They are often pop culture responses to current events. For example, a meme of Senator Bernie Sanders went viral in 2021 after he appeared at President Joe Biden's inauguration in a winter parka and oversized, hand-knitted woollen mittens. The image of Sanders was photoshopped into historical pictures and other unusual backgrounds to create humorous juxtapositions. And the humorous memes proliferated.

Memes can also have serious social implications. At the outset of the #MeToo movement, China blocked the campaign's hashtags. To express solidarity or share their own experiences of sexual harassment, the people of China had to find a way around the censorship. Rice Bunny memes, often featuring a cartoon-like bowl of rice and bunny, started circulating online. In Chinese, the words *rice* and *bunny* are "mi tu."

Warhol's use of images from pop culture to convey a message, memes also require creativity and capture a cultural moment in time.

Moving Images

Memes are not always static posts. They may also be presented as videos. And although social media users have had the ability to post videos on platforms like Facebook and X (formerly known as Twitter), videos have been turbocharged on TikTok.

According to the *Washington Post*, TikTok has grown faster than any app ever. As of 2023, it had 1.67 billion users worldwide. And in the United States, people view an average of eighty minutes of TikTok videos a day—that is more time than is spent on Facebook and Instagram combined. This has led to a trend to incorporate motion graph-

WORDS IN CONTEXT

augmented reality: Technology commonly known as AR that superimposes digital images such as text or graphics atop reality when viewed through a smart device

ics, animations, and augmented reality (AR) in designs as a highly visual way to tell a story.

AR is especially conducive to the art of graphic design. Content can be made more sensory, lifelike, and immersive as users interact with the design in a simulated real-world, real-time scenario. Contributing writer Samantha Spiro explains on Linearity, a resource website for digital designers:

> Augmented reality (AR) can be used in graphic design to create interactive and immersive user experiences. . . . AR can also create interactive posters, brochures, and other marketing materials that provide additional information or experiences when viewed through an AR-enabled device. . . . In short, AR expands the possibilities for graphic design.[8]

AI and Artificial Art

Technology like AR continues to revolutionize the graphic art industry, particularly with the acceleration of AI. Digital art and design software programs have advanced so much that today's artists do not necessarily need art skills. They can create art in the style of other, more well-known artists with just a click of a button. This is even easier now with AI tools such as ChatGPT that has "learned" all these techniques from combing through the internet's storehouses of copyrighted and unlicensed material. But such abilities have also created problems. There have already been many book illustrators with iconic styles whose livelihoods are being threatened by those who are creating work very similar to theirs by using AI tools to mimic those characteristic styles.

Michael Whelan, a science-fiction and fantasy illustrator who has created covers for novels by authors such as Stephen King and Ray Bradbury, is one such person. In a report from November 2023 Erik Ofgang of the *New York Times* explained, "Over the past few months, users working with A.I. art generators have created hundreds of images in Whelan's style that were slightly altered knockoffs of his work, he said, forcing him to devote considerable time and resources to getting the images removed from the web."[9]

And some book publishers, particularly independent or smaller presses, have been using AI-generated cover designs to save money. This practice is having a direct effect on the incomes of graphic artists. There have even been some instances of AI-created book covers for works of some high-profile authors. *New York Times* best-selling author Christopher Paolini's 2022 novel *Fractal Noise* was discovered to have an AI-generated cover. A spokesperson for Paolini's publisher, Tor Books, said it had only learned after the fact that the cover may have been created using AI. "The funny thing is, in so much science fiction it was theorized that robots, A.I., all this stuff was going to take over the drudgery, the hard labor, and free up humans to do creative work," Paolini told the *New York Times*. "Instead the A.I. is taking over the creative work, and we're all stuck doing the hard labor."[10] Many graphic designers are concerned that AI will threaten their livelihoods and could potentially replace them. Afterall, if computers can create art through prompts, there is a fear that consumers will simply turn to AI for logos, posters, and other graphic arts rather than employing living artists.

However, not everyone believes that AI will take over the graphic art industry. Some industry professionals see AI as beneficial, providing tools that could help artists enhance their designs. At the same time, these professionals believe that entirely AI-generated designs will lack personalization and result in a sameness of design. They maintain that artists and designers will always be needed, specifically because of the "humanness" of their work. Lucy Marino of the magazine *Graphic Design USA* says that "human feel" cannot be duplicated. "As AI and automation shake up creative industries," she writes, "qualities like emotional intelligence and empathy are gaining importance. That's because while machines can crunch numbers and analyze data, they can't read a room, take a risk they weren't programmed to take or form human connections. In the creative world, understanding what makes people tick often drives success."[11]

The Future of Graphic Arts

Design software and the internet have reshaped graphic arts, but the innovation has not stopped. AI and machine learning are providing ways for graphic artists to write code that prompts computers to create "new" images. If an artist's image is incomplete, AI tools can also finish off the work by again drawing from existing images that are similar and suggesting a way to fuse them into the incomplete image. As Das asserts, "Technology will have a major impact in the coming years. Designers can use natural language descriptions to generate user interfaces, or they can use machine learning to auto-complete designs just like predictive text on your phone's keyboard."[12]

Whether used to tell a story, mark occasions, create pleasing imagery, or chart personal growth, graphic arts have remained a part of every culture. Some argue that our ability to create art is what separates humans from other species. The desire to create has never stopped; humans have continued to advance their arts as well as other aspects of their cultures. As with other aspects of civilization, technology has aided the spread of graphic arts. But it is still the individual artists who have the vision and the know-how to bring those visions to life.

Visual Storytelling

Graphic arts have many purposes. They can entertain, decorate, and inform. Many tell a story by using imagery to evoke emotions or encourage viewers to think about an issue. Graphic designers who work in advertising also motivate or inspire an audience to buy products, often by creating visual narratives or referencing traditional ones that already have certain emotions and mindsets attached to them.

Visual storytelling through graphic arts is everywhere. It is on food packaging, billboards, subway walls, websites, and phone apps. And the style or medium the graphic artist uses to tell a particular story will depend on that story's goal—that is, on the tone or message the artist hopes to communicate. According to Magipik, the screen name of an author on Medium, a website for writers:

> Humans are visual creatures, and we are naturally drawn to images and visuals that tell a story. . . . Firstly, visual design helps to establish the tone and mood of your story. The choice of colors, typography, and imagery can evoke specific emotions and set the stage for the narrative. . . . Secondly, visual design aids in clarifying complex concepts or ideas. Sometimes, words alone are not enough to effectively communicate a message. Visuals can simplify complex information, making it easier for the audience to understand and retain the information being presented.[13]

The graphic art component may be a painting, a photograph, or a cartoon—or a mash-up of all three. It may be rendered in traditional art mediums such as pencil or paint, or it may be created digitally to simulate one of those mediums. Mediums may be combined as well, such as pencil and ink or a soft watercolor wash over the top of a photograph. But whether it is a political message spray-painted on the side of a building, an engaging cover photograph that entices a reader to buy a book, an illustrated map to help someone navigate a subway system, or a digital advertising campaign intended to sell more cheese, there is a story built into these images.

Vinnie Wong is a content specialist at Piktochart, an online content creator. According to Wong, 65 percent of the population are visual learners who benefit from visual storytelling. "An effective image can convey a complex idea instantly, sparking emotions or reactions that long-form content alone may fail to ignite," Wong says. "[Images] can change the entire experience and create lasting impressions by appealing directly to our senses. The aspects of visual learning—seeing, interpreting, understanding—allow for deeper connections with the material presented."[14]

Graphic designers who work with food packaging create visual narratives that tap into people's emotions and experiences. In this way, they hope to inspire consumers to buy a certain product.

Graphic Artists at Work

Using art to tell a story is a talent. Some graphic artists may have gone to school to learn their craft, while others are self-taught. Graphic artists are also highly creative. And they express their creativity in distinct ways. Some create using traditional methods, sketching ideas with mediums such as pencil, charcoal, or ink. As they refine their ideas, they may add color using pencil crayons, colored inks, or perhaps paint. They may play with the composition as well as the colors and mediums until they formulate a strong idea that conveys exactly what they want to say. Some artists continue with these methods until they have the finalized art. But others may scan their original artwork into an art-based software program on a digital device such as a computer, smartphone, or tablet. Once the art is downloaded, they may manipulate it digitally. They can also

But Is It Art?

Modern-day graffiti or street art is often not seen as art but as vandalism and something to be removed. Heather Mac Donald, a fellow at the Manhattan Institute, stated in 2014, "Graffiti is always vandalism. By definition it is committed without permission on another person's property, in an adolescent display of entitlement." But others believe there is value in the tagging and the spray-painted images. Banksy's work has commanded large sums of money, and owners of buildings tagged with a Banksy original are often overjoyed by the valuable prize left for them.

Still, not every piece of street art is a Banksy, and a lot of stickers, graffiti, and other forms of do-it-yourself creations are scoured off buildings and railway cars by owners who do not like their property being defaced. Even though many works by street artists are now housed in exhibition halls, it is the many temporary pieces encountered in the wild that seem to give voice to unresolved social ills, political disagreements, the joys of creating, and the value of community. As Banksy has said of street art, "If our civilization was destroyed, future generations would piece together life in the 21st century using only the scrawlings on our subway walls."

Heather Mac Donald, "Graffiti Is Always Vandalism," *New York Times*, December 4, 2014. www.nytimes.com.

Quoted in David Fickling, "Cave Paintings Are Graffiti by Prehistoric Yobs," *The Independent* (London), February 26, 2006. www.independent.co.uk.

add animation or some non–graphic art elements such as video or music to complete the work.

> ## WORDS IN CONTEXT
>
> **composition: The way artwork elements such as shapes, lines, light, and color are arranged**

Graphic artists who strictly work digitally have a similar process. However, digital artists usually sketch their ideas directly onto a tablet instead of paper or canvas. And then they play around with form and color by using various digital tools. They can instantly switch out colors, change a layout, or imitate a specific art style or medium. Working digitally allows an artist to work faster and make changes much more easily, with no cleanup required. It also allows the artist's work to be portable. Digital artists can share their work with others easily—and immediately—no matter where they are in the world, with no need to print. And with today's advancements in AI, artists can create computer-generated graphic art in minutes, just by inputting some data.

Regardless of how the graphic art is created—traditionally, digitally, or a hybrid of the two—effective visual storytelling has several things in common. "Whether it's children's picture books or a brand's content marketing strategy," Wong says, "the best narratives follow the same principles and employ the same elements. Imagery, composition, colors, and typography are all essential components of this art form. Visual storytelling works when these elements are combined together."[15]

> ## WORDS IN CONTEXT
>
> **matrix: A physical surface that can be manipulated to hold ink, enabling image transfer to a surface such as paper or canvas**

Illustrative Purposes

Graphic artists span many industries. They might work in fields such as education, publishing, film, video games, fashion, product packaging, and advertising. And except for graphic designers, most graphic artists work on their own—particularly illustrators.

Illustration is probably the largest area of graphic arts next to graphic design. Its main purpose is to interpret, explain, illustrate, or enhance text (if used) across multiple formats. Formats such as photographs, drawings, and paintings are often used in the illustration of posters, greeting cards, magazines, newspapers, comics, books, film credits, and video games. It is important that illustrations be clear and intentional in their purpose, as well as engaging, to attract the viewer.

Illustrators often specialize or have niche areas of interest. For example, editorial illustrators usually work under the guidance of an editor or art director in the publishing industry. These art-

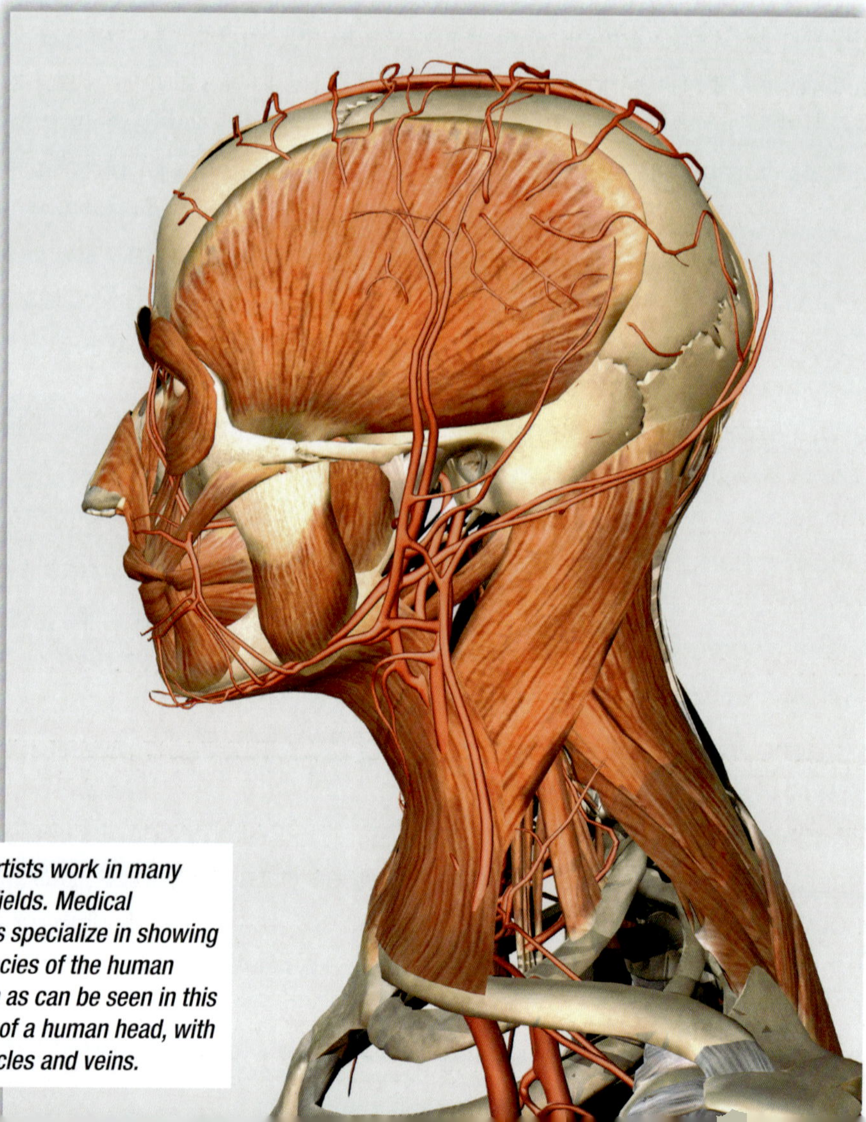

Graphic artists work in many different fields. Medical illustrators specialize in showing the intricacies of the human body such as can be seen in this side view of a human head, with neck muscles and veins.

ists provide illustrations—or create a visual narrative—for newspapers, magazines, and books. Children's book illustrators illustrate stories. Sometimes the illustrations match the narrative, and sometimes illustrators share their own visual interpretation. Sometimes illustrators work directly with the author of the text, but usually they work with an art director who acts as a liaison between the illustrator and author. Comic book and graphic novel illustrators work similarly to children's book illustrators. Much like they do in children's books, these illustrators create visuals to entertain and engage the audience in support of the written story.

Illustrators can specialize in various subjects. For example, medical illustrators create illustrations for medical books, and science illustrators for science books. Both fields are specialized, and the illustrators need training in the subject matter to create the highly complex and detailed visuals. Fashion illustrators work in the fashion industry. Some may simply illustrate magazine articles or books, but many work in advertising. Fashion illustrators need an interest in fashion as well as to be current on fashion trends. And courtroom illustrators require quick drawing skills. These artists illustrate what is happening during a trial when photography and video are banned from proceedings.

Product illustrators straddle two graphic art formats: illustration and graphic design. They illustrate the packaging for various products. The illustrations may also be used for a brand's promotional materials, such as brochures, websites, and advertising.

The Art of Printmaking

Printmaking is another form of illustration that also can be found in many industries. During the printmaking process, graphic artists create what is called a matrix. A matrix is created by etching, engraving, or carving images on a surface such as rock, wood, metal, or linoleum. After preparing and painting the surface of the matrix, the artists transfer the image they've created onto another 2-D surface, such as paper or fabric. Some artists use a hand roller or a printing press to achieve an even impression. An artist can make multiple copies of the same original work, which is why printmaking is most often used for poster art.

Screen printing is a type of printmaking. However, screen printers create a stencil of their design, which is placed between a mesh screen and another surface like paper or fabric. Ink is then drawn over the screen with a squeegee, pushing the ink through the mesh onto the paper or fabric except where blocked by the stencil. Screen printing may be done by hand or machine and is most often used for mass poster or clothing designs.

Printmaking has been around for a long time. Peggy Carouthers, a writer for *Art & Object* magazine, says:

> Printmaking is one of the oldest human art forms. Not only have engravings on bones and rocks survived from prehistoric times, but engraved designs have been used to transfer and duplicate images since as far back as 3000 BCE, when Sumerians used cuneiform [a system of ancient writing in the Middle East] engravings to create relief impressions on clay tablets.[16]

WORDS IN CONTEXT

pop art: An art movement arising in the 1950s that used easily reproducible images from pop culture to undermine the elitist notion of high art and make artworks available to the masses

Certainly, printmaking techniques have evolved over the centuries. Modern printmakers' ability to produce multiple copies with ease ensured the value of printmaking to advertising and consumer culture. And that seemingly endless reproducibility of images and their commercialization became a way for pop artists in the mid-twentieth century to democratize art. San Francisco designer and photographer Monica Galvan explains:

> Primarily a British and American cultural phenomenon that gained traction in the late 1950s and 1960s, Pop Art was

> named by art critic Lawrence Alloway because of the way it glorified popular culture and elevated commonplace, often unremarkable objects to iconic statuses. The pop art movement began as a revolt against the dominant approaches to art, culture, and traditional views on what art should be. Sources of inspiration ranged from Hollywood movies, advertising, product packaging, pop music, and comic books, rejecting the pretensions of "high art" in favor of bold, graphic printmaking.[17]

Pop art was also a reaction to the increasing postwar consumerism. Its style was used heavily throughout all forms of mass media, which the movement also scorned. However, the pop art movement was not without controversy. Not everyone considered it art, and many critics thought it vulgar.

Taking It to the Streets

Street art is another form of graphic art that attempts to democratize art. Its goal is to make art accessible to everyone. However, street art has a couple of unique challenges that other types of graphic arts lack. Most street artists have a desire to display their art to the public, usually in an urban environment, in a way that is freely accessible. But street art—such as graffiti, chalk art, and murals—is for the most part illegal. That does not stop street artists, especially those with something to say, from putting up their work on subway and railway cars, abandoned buildings, or other surfaces they do not own.

American street artist Shepard Fairey—whose work has been compared to that of pop artist Andy Warhol—is one of those artists. "Galleries and museums have their place but they shouldn't be the only venues for people to experience art," Fairey tells the Art Story, a nonprofit art resource website. "I think of myself as an artist, but most people categorize me as a street artist because I do a lot of public art, with and without permission. I consider myself an artist with an agenda to democratise art. I want to reach people through as many platforms as possible."[18]

However, another issue with street art is its impermanence. The artworks sometimes disappear as fast as they are created. Of course, in the case of chalk art, it washes away with the rain or is worn away by foot traffic. But graffiti and wall murals are often removed by the authorities or owners of the cityscape surfaces that street artists turn into their canvases.

Having his art destroyed is a common occurrence for Banksy, the anonymous British street artist whose reputation has made his surviving art worth millions. Disguised as a cleaner, Banksy created a painting inside a London subway car in July 2020 encouraging people to mask up during the COVID-19 pandemic. Banksy followed up by posting a video of himself in the act on Instagram. However, by the time the video was released, officials from the London Underground had already scrubbed away what they deemed vandalism, unaware of its famous creator.

Banksy's street art has also been the target of theft. In December 2023 a Banksy piece featuring three drones painted over the word "Stop" on a London-area stop sign was stolen in front of a group of photo-snapping fans less than an hour after Banksy posted about it on social media.

Making a Mark

Like Banksy, many graphic artists use social media to promote their work and stay relevant. However, most social media platforms are so crowded that it is hard to stand out online. But graphic artists need to stay on top of new trends as well as the latest art techniques and technologies.

Although some graphic artists work full time for various companies, many are freelance, or self-employed. Freelance artists have traditionally made a name for themselves by creating a portfolio—samples of their work—and sharing it physically with potential clients. Today, however, an artist's work may be posted on online industry websites or visual social media platforms like Instagram and TikTok.

Andy Warhol's Soup Cans

American Andy Warhol is probably the most well known artist associated with the pop art movement. Warhol, who started out as a commercial illustrator of products such as shoes, was inspired by something most Americans stocked in their cupboards—Campbell's soup. Warhol created individual screen prints of the labels of each of the brand's thirty-two flavors. The art world was less than warm in its reception. Only a handful of prints sold for about a hundred dollars each. After Warhol died unexpectedly in 1987, a gallery did a retrospective of the art series that renewed interest in the pop art prints.

Alexandra Peers, a writer with CNN, says, "It helped the soup artworks' value that it became a hugely popular print series, and that it had two warring interpretations by critics. Some argued the work was an acrid but intelligent criticism of mass-production, even of capitalism, while others saw a more comforting wall of soup, more about America and post-war options and prosperity."

Today the collection is valued at $15 million and is housed at New York's Museum of Modern Art. Warhol went on to create prints of screen legends Elvis Presley and Marilyn Monroe—one of which sold for $195 million in 2024.

Alexandra Peers, "Why Campbell Soup Hated, Then Embraced, Andy Warhol's Soup Can Painting," CNN, July 29, 2022. www.cnn.com.

In a 2013 interview with *Smithsonian* magazine, Banksy celebrated the fact that he can communicate directly with his fans and followers, despite his anonymity. "There's a whole new audience out there, and it's never been easier to sell [one's art]. You don't have to go to college, drag 'round a portfolio, mail off transparencies to snooty galleries . . . all you need now is a few ideas and a broadband connection. This is the first time the essentially bourgeois world of art has belonged to the people."[19]

Type Matters

Banksy also uses text in some of his art to help reinforce his message. And graphic artists who combine images with text know that the text is as important as any of the other elements of the artwork.

Typography is not just about selecting a pleasing font. The font, like an image, sends a message, so it is important that the right font, in the right size, in the right color, is chosen. Even the spacing of the individual letters and the number of different fonts used should be considered carefully. "Effective typography ensures clarity, sets tone, and emphasizes important messages," Vinnie Wong says. "As part of brand storytelling, it conveys mood and tone, giving voice to your tale in ways words alone cannot."[20]

Famed Italian graphic designer Massimo Vignelli (1931–2014) was known for clarity and simplicity in his typography. A product

Italian graphic designer Massimo Vignelli's New York subway system map made getting around on the city's subways much easier. The map featured color-coded routes, and dots represented subway stops.

of the pre-digital age, Vignelli was an inspiration to generations of designers. He often created his own typography by shaving off bits of letters to get the form and spacing he wanted.

Vignelli is most known for the design of the 1972 map and signage for the New York City subway system. Prior to 1972 it was a nightmare for people trying to find their way around the city—especially for those who did not speak English. Vignelli created a simple, color-coded map with dots representing the subway stops. Although the map has since been updated, his signage system featuring his unique typography is still in use today.

A Continuing Narrative

The art of visual storytelling has changed over the decades and centuries. Graphic art has taken massive steps, particularly since the digital revolution. Gone are the days of actually cutting and pasting artwork, having to start over every time something needs to be changed, or actually trimming fonts to create the look and feel that one desires. However, what has not changed is the desire of graphic artists to tell a story through images.

Chapter Three

Graphic Design and the Art of Selling

Graphic design is a category of graphic art similar to illustration. Both art forms use images and sometimes typography. Both art forms focus on telling a story that communicates a message and induces an emotion. However, graphic design is often closely linked with advertising. Therefore, graphic design most commonly persuades its viewer to buy a product or service. "Since graphic design aims to inspire action," Upwork, a freelance job marketplace, states, "the creative process works differently than it does for illustration. A graphic designer has to research the design ecosystem and carefully select the typography, images, fonts, colors, and shapes they want to use so the design can come together to have a powerful impact on the audience."[21]

To achieve that memorable impression, graphic designers create a brand, or a visual identity, that represents a company or product and its values. For example, a pair of golden arches, a swoosh, an apple with a bite out of it—these logos for McDonald's, Nike, and Apple Inc., respectively, are some of the most iconic logos ever designed. The symbols, though often abstract, have come to represent the values, endurance, and corporate and even social identity of their companies. And even more importantly, these logos are instantly recognizable. So, whether selling a hamburger, a sneaker, or a smartphone, graphic design must communicate its message with just a glance.

Graphic Designers at Work

Beyond devising corporate logos, graphic designers create visual concepts for other marketing tools, such as brochures, product packaging, and websites. Some designers work for universities, nonprofit organizations, and other institutions that might be selling an image rather than goods and services. Regardless of the employer, graphic designers try to create a recognizable and unique brand by balancing multiple design elements, such as color, images, illustrations, composition, and typography.

> **WORDS IN CONTEXT**
>
> **brand: How a company expresses its identity to create a desired perception among customers**

In today's rapidly evolving digital world, graphic design has become a combination of art and technology. And although some designers might sketch out their initial ideas by hand with traditional tools such as a pencil and paper, most use digital tools. Digital illustration, photo editing, and layout software help designers do their jobs more efficiently, so it is crucial that designers are up-to-date on the latest design technology. It is also important that designers are aware of design trends. As in the fashion industry, what was trendy last year may look tired and dated this year, so graphic designers must be current to stay relevant. They need to know what is hot and what is not.

Most graphic designers obtain a diploma or a degree in their field. Once completed, they may intern with another designer to help build their portfolio and client list. Some designers work independently and are self-employed, but the majority work in industries such as advertising, marketing, or public relations. Such jobs are usually collaborative, and designers may work as part of a design team that includes writers, editors, and art directors.

The Nike swoosh is a classic example of how graphic designers create a brand, or visual identity, that represents a company or product. The swoosh is instantly recognizable to people around the world.

Graphic design is split into two formats: print and digital. Some designers specialize in print design, which includes product packaging, business cards, and brochures. Others focus on digital design creating logos, websites, or social media posts. But whether print or digital, an effective design needs to communicate a message—one that is hopefully understood instantaneously and that overcomes any possible language barrier.

Capturing People's Attention

People are bombarded with ads constantly. And the most effective logos or advertising campaigns are those that provide strong brand recognition and stimulate an emotional reaction that motivates the viewer to buy. It is a real art to create a design that both encapsulates a brand and translates its values and message—especially when one only has seconds to grab a person's attention.

The average attention span of humans has declined over time. In fact, a much-quoted 2015 study claimed it dropped from 12 seconds to 8.25 over the five years prior—which is reportedly less than the attention span of a goldfish. In the age of social media, good designers are aware of how fleeting a viewer's interest is. However, they recognize that expressing information visually is still the superior method of communication for the human brain.

According to the National Library of Medicine, a US government agency, humans process visual data faster than other data. "The human brain processes images 60,000 times faster than text, and 90 percent of information transmitted to the brain is visual,"[22] the agency claims. Furthermore, the Massachusetts Institute of Technology has established that humans can process images and determine their meaning in as little as thirteen milliseconds. To put it in context, the blink of an eye lasts anywhere from one hundred to three hundred milliseconds.

Plus, it is not just the part of the brain that processes visual information that is activated when one looks at an image. Studies show that the part of the brain that processes emotions also lights up—the part of the brain that is susceptible to storytelling. This is why visual storytelling remains an effective design strategy.

The Power of Storytelling

One corporation whose logo is instantly recognized and needs no translation is Coca-Cola. The red-and-white script logo, substantially unchanged since the late 1800s, is one of the most internationally recognizable logos in the world. Part of its success is due to storytelling. The soft drink's successful advertising campaigns link the product with positive emotions and shared human experiences, particularly with Coca-Cola's Christmas campaigns. According to the Because of Marketing website:

In the world of festive marketing, one brand has stood the test of time, becoming synonymous with the holiday season: Coca-Cola. The soft drink giant's journey into the hearts of consumers during Christmas began in 1930 when an illustrator named Haddon Sundblom crafted a warm and friendly image of Santa Claus enjoying a Coke. Little did they know, this creative decision would shape the company's holiday marketing for decades to come.[23]

Coca-Cola's ability to link its product to pleasurable emotions is the work of designers. Sundblom's Santa image, for example,

Coca-Cola's ad campaigns have long relied on storytelling that links the product with positive emotions and shared human experiences. This is especially evident in the company's Christmas ads, such as this one from 1959.

has remained prevalent in Coke's marketing even as more recent graphic designers have reworked the imagery, making it new yet still nostalgic for customers. This has created a legacy of images and heartwarming feelings that have kept Coke fans loyal.

The authors of the *Adobe Express* blog reiterate this power of successful marketing when they write, "Remarkable or impactful advertising campaigns, whether in print or digital form, tend to share a commonality: the ability to captivate, inspire, and resonate with audiences. Successful ads don't just promote products, but engage viewers well beyond a passing glance, forming a lasting impression and positive perception of a company or service's brand."[24]

Visual Identity

Branding is about creating an overall visual story or identity for a company, person, or product. The goal of branding is to promote a positive image of the subject through its tone, mission, values, and imagery such as logos, commercials, and print advertisements. The graphic designer hopes to communicate the brand's less tangible qualities—like trust, quality, fun, charity, and concern for customers—in an attempt to stand out from its competitors.

> **WORDS IN CONTEXT**
>
> **visual identity: The visual elements—such as logo, values, tone, colors, images, and typography—that make a brand stand out from competitors**

Award-winning branding specialist Jessica Walsh, who started creating websites at age eleven, is one of the most in-demand graphic designers today. Known for her funky, vibrant designs, Walsh believes the key to branding is "finding your weird." Walsh tells Kelsie Rimmer of Envato Elements, a graphic design website:

> We believe every brand has something weird, different, or unique that's their most valuable asset. . . . We help each brand "find their weird," discover who they are, and develop our work around that. . . . When your brand looks like

everyone else, it's difficult to differentiate in the competitive landscape and create something memorable and timeless. A great brand is like a great person: genuine and honest about who they are and unafraid to show their true colors.[25]

Logos are a key part of branding. A logo is simply a graphic symbol that represents the company, but a successful logo captures the identity of the brand and separates it from similar brands. "You want to stand out in your industry but it should fit that industry," asserts Andrew Warner, creative director for Maverick, a premier branding and marketing agency. For example, "a toy shop's logo should be fun and energetic, an internet security firm should transmit trust and solidity."[26]

In addition, a good logo can arouse an emotional response and evoke memories, as illustrated by the Coca-Cola logo, which has stayed virtually the same for over a century. Cartier, the luxury jewelry brand, has a similar story. Its classic, elegant script logo has stayed the same since it was created in 1900. And although KFC has updated its logo and changed its name from Kentucky Fried Chicken to distance itself from the now negative perception of *fried*, the company has adhered to the same red, white, and black color combination since the 1950s, helping its brand recognition. As KFC and McDonald's know, color can also play an important role in devising the right logo. According to color psychology, yellow and red stimulate appetite.

Having said all of the above, however, it is important not to make a logo be too complex or try to say too much. And that is where the real art of graphic design comes into play. American graphic designer Paul Rand (1914–1996) was considered one of the best at designing logos, and he inspired many generations of designers. Known for his sleek, stripped-down designs, he once said, "A logo derives its meaning from the quality of the thing it symbolises, not the other way around. A logo is less important than the product it signifies; what it means is more important than what it looks like."[27]

A Little Something Extra

Graphic designers often add elements to their logos to enhance their brand or create buzz. For example, the Amazon logo features an arrow from the first "a" in "amazon" to the "z," indicating that Amazon sells everything from A to Z. The arrow also doubles as a smile, suggesting customer satisfaction. Baskin-Robbins has "31" hidden in its logo for how many ice cream flavors it originally sold—one for every day of the month.

FedEx's logo was arrived at by chance. While sifting through hundreds of logo designs, Lindon Leader, the senior designer at Landor, the company charged with rebranding FedEx, made a discovery. "If you put a lower-case 'x' to the right of a capital 'E' [in the word *Ex*], you can begin to see a hint of an arrow," he notes. Recalling his excitement, he adds "If I could develop this concept of an arrow, it could be promoted as a symbol for speed and precision, both FedEx communicative attributes." A new font was designed to make the arrow more prominent, leading CNN to include the FedEx logo as one of "20 designs that defined the modern world."

Quoted in Andrew Adam Newman, "Logo Big or Go Home: How FedEx's Secret Arrow Was Created Accidentally," Retail Brew, October 7, 2022. www.retailbrew.com.

Aligning with Audience Values

Beyond the logo itself, consumers are attracted to brands that purport to have similar values as they do. A company that knows who its audience is and what it values can use that information—hopefully authentically—to provide fuel for its ad campaigns. The marketing of the personal care brand Dove is a great example of this strategy. After surveying more than three thousand women in ten countries in 2004, Dove found only 2 percent thought themselves attractive. To highlight and counteract unattainable beauty standards, Dove launched the Dove Campaign for Real Beauty, a multimedia campaign using print, digital, social media, and billboard ads. This campaign, considered one of the most successful ever, urges women—of all shapes and sizes—to embrace their bodies.

Uber Eats employed technology in one of its campaigns to highlight one of its company values, inclusivity. In 2023 the food delivery company created a series of digital billboards in the United Kingdom aimed at Muslims marking Ramadan. Ramadan, a month of prayer, gratitude, and reflection, requires Muslims to fast until sunset each evening before taking part in iftar, the end-of-the-day meal. The Uber Eats monthlong digital campaign featured vibrant images of Muslim food with the headline "Iftar incoming," followed by the time of sunset adjusted to the location of the billboard. Below that was a call to action: "Schedule your sunset food or grocery delivery," simply followed by the company's name. Attempting to relate to a targeted customer base—including one often ignored in Western advertising—is a way to attract potential buyers who might feel the company is speaking to them.

Adding Interactive Elements

Another way to add value to a brand is by adding an interactive element to a design. For example, Swedish home goods king IKEA included a pregnancy test strip as part of a 2018 magazine ad for a baby's crib. The accompanying headline implored: "Peeing on this ad may change your life." If the pregnancy test was positive, a coupon code was revealed for 50 percent off the price of the crib.

IKEA has also experimented with augmented reality. It created a design app that allows people to virtually place IKEA furniture in their homes through the magic of augmented reality. The IKEA Place app scans the customer's room, then customers can drag and drop scaled-to-fit furniture into the space, allowing them to see what it might look like.

Atypical Typography

Typography played a role in all the above ad campaigns. And whether the fonts used are custom made or digitally generated, the importance of creative, well-placed typography cannot be overstated in graphic design. "Typography has the ability to provoke emotions, communicate messages, build hierarchy, and improve the overall aesthetics of a design," design writer Magipik explains on Medium. "It goes beyond just choosing and arranging typefaces."[28]

David Carson, an American graphic designer who came to prominence in the late 1990s, is one whose work with typogra-

Typography can be used to convey messages and elicit a variety of emotional responses. In this image, the same message comes across differently depending on the fonts and design.

phy involves much more than typefaces. A former competitive surfer once ranked ninth in the world, Carson has won hundreds of awards and accolades for his chaotic, guerrilla-meets-grunge style print design featuring overlapping images and oversized fonts in grid-free formats, most notably as art director of *Ray Gun*, an alternative-music magazine. Carson, who is considered the godfather of the grunge design aesthetic, was once ranked one of the top five influential graphic designers of the era by *Graphic Design USA* magazine, alongside design royalty Milton Glaser, Saul Bass, Paul Rand, and Massimo Vignelli.

Carson, who is still breaking design rules today and working with some of the top brands in the world, sees letters as art and uses them as one would use images, or perhaps paint, to evoke a response. During his 2003 TED talk, Carson said, “I'm a big

A Clever Apology Restores Trust in KFC

What happens when a brand messes up? Smart brands acknowledge their mistakes and use them as a springboard for an iconic apology campaign. For example, in 2018 most of the United Kingdom's nine hundred KFC restaurants were forced to close temporarily when they ran out of chicken due to distribution problems. KFC reportedly lost $1 million a day, and angry customers took to social media. Tahir Abbas of *Change Management Insight* explains:

> Social media platforms quickly erupted with posts from disappointed and frustrated customers, expressing their disbelief at the absence of KFC's famous fried chicken. The crisis intensified as the media caught wind of the story, further amplifying the negative publicity surrounding the situation. The impact of this crisis was significant on multiple fronts. Not only did it disrupt the day-to-day operations of KFC restaurants, leading to financial losses, but it also tarnished the brand's reputation.

In response, KFC created a brilliant—and hilarious—ad campaign featuring an image of an empty bucket of KFC with an apology underneath. However, on closer inspection, the letters of the company's iconic logo had been rearranged from "KFC" to "FCK." The ad went viral, easing the public relations mess and restoring trust in the brand.

Tahir Abbas, "KFC Crisis Management Case Study: Preparing for the Unexpected," *Change Management Insight*, May 28, 2023. https://changemanagementinsight.com.

believer in the emotion of design, and the message that's sent before somebody begins to read, before they get the rest of the information; what is the emotional response they get to the product, to the story, to the painting—whatever it is."[29]

Digital Evolution

Along with the age of the internet, websites and virtual storefronts started popping up online. Graphic designers were suddenly in high demand to design the aesthetics—the overall look—for websites. Websites need to be user-friendly, easy to navigate, and cohesive in their branding. Graphic designers use attractive colors, fonts, and images to attract visitors. They also put these elements into a layout that helps users find what they are looking for.

The need for branded content increased alongside advances in technology that saw the rise of social media and other digital platforms such as mobile phones. The decided swing to digital from print media meant designers needed to create not only effective and aesthetically pleasing content but also responsive content that adjusts to multiple platforms, be it a computer, a tablet, or a phone. It is the job of graphic designers to ensure that these applications are successful in conveying the message of the brand and providing a satisfying experience for visitors.

An Unknown Future

Some members of the design industry are concerned about the future of graphic design. And their concerns are not just about the unknowns surrounding the burgeoning AI industry. With the rise of digital design and the increasing demise of print design, designers worry about a drastic reduction of work, since it now takes considerably less time to do the same amount of work. However, others feel there always will be new technologies to learn and conquer, particularly as technology is advancing at a more rapid pace.

It has been almost six hundred years since the invention of the printing press, when the art form of graphic design really took hold. However, it has only been a few decades since the introduction of digital design. And with the explosion of AI, no one is sure what the graphic design industry will look like in another decade. But graphic designers are creative. They are adaptive by nature and solution oriented, trained to think outside the box. Plus, there will always be something that needs to be marketed.

Chapter Four

Legendary Graphic Artists

Some say art acts as a mirror reflecting culture during a specific time and place in history. Society's collective memory of a notable artwork can be so strong that even if an individual cannot name the artist of the work, that person can usually define its era just by its style.

Others wonder whether society is not just reflected by art but also shaped by it. According to Medium, "By understanding and appreciating art's ability to mirror and shape society, we develop a deeper appreciation for its enduring significance. Art remains a fundamental tool for cultural preservation, social change, and fostering dialogue, crystallizing the essence of human expression and creativity."[30]

Norman Rockwell: America's Trusted Storyteller

Graphic art is no exception. And no graphic artist both mirrored and shaped American society more than New York illustrator Norman Rockwell. A successful commercial artist for iconic products such as Jell-O, Skippy peanut butter, and Coca-Cola, Rockwell is most known for more than three hundred magazine covers he painted for the *Saturday Evening Post*, an influence that spanned five decades. He was a master visual storyteller, and his paintings appeared on the cover of the *Saturday Evening Post* from 1916 to

1963, reflecting American ideals to Americans. According to the Norman Rockwell Museum:

> Responsible for helping to shape the perception of American society and culture in the 20th century, Norman Rockwell possessed a distinct ability to create works of art that evoke a strong emotional response. Many of the emotions drawn from the viewer are memories of formative events from their own lives, nostalgia toward a time long gone, or a feeling of Americans collectively united through war-time patriotism.[31]

Rockwell's earlier images, particularly his covers for the *Saturday Evening Post*, are of simpler times. He painted everyday situations. Boys playing baseball, young love, and heartwarming images of families gathered around the Thanksgiving table emphasized a longing for a shared sense of innocence. Rockwell's April 24, 1926, cover titled *Little Spooners* features a young boy with his arm slung around an equally young girl who is clutching a couple of daisies while they watch the sunset. *The Soda Fountain*, from August 26, 1953, shows three lovesick girls sitting at a soda counter enjoying sodas and the undivided attention of the young man working behind the counter. Although Rockwell's initial covers were somewhat idyllic and quite nostalgic—Rockwellian, as they became known—by the 1960s they portrayed a very different America, one much less innocent, having been marked by war, politics, and civil rights protests. After Rockwell left the *Saturday Evening Post*, he created a memorable painting that appeared in *Look* magazine in 1964 titled *The Problem We All Live With*. It featured six-year-old Ruby Bridges on her first day of kindergarten. She was the first African American child to attend a newly desegregated school in the US South, and Rockwell depicts her with the four White US marshals who accompanied her on that historic day. Along a wall in the background of

Ruby Bridges holds a print of the Norman Rockwell painting *The Problem We All Live With*. She was the first African American child to attend an all-White elementary school in the South. Rockwell depicted her actions on that historic day.

the painting was a chalked racial slur and the remains of a tomato thrown by the unseen White crowd that stood against desegregation. "Rockwell was at times a documentarian and a mythmaker," the Norman Rockwell Museum states. "By transforming a blank canvas into a portrayal of a young African-American girl courageously enduring a hate-filled crowd on her walk to school, Rockwell depicted Ruby Bridges as a modern day Joan of Arc."[32]

The artwork, which appeared as a wordless two-page spread, was met with immediate controversy. Rockwell, who died in 1978, was both praised and vilified for his visual statement. Many of his fans wished for a return of Rockwell's earlier, sentimental work, which has often been described as representing the American dream.

Milton Glaser: Defining a City

Milton Glaser is another American graphic artist whose art undeniably pinpoints a time—sometimes with just a glance. Like

Rockwell, he gave shape to America's cultural conversation in the 1960s and 1970s. And he did it primarily as a commercial artist, whether selling record albums, TV shows, or even a city. Glaser's work—stylized, sophisticated, sleek images often contrasted with bold, sometimes psychedelic, colors—defined a generation. "No art director's work was more influential or instantly identifiable than that of Milton Glaser," Adam Gopnik writes in the *New Yorker*. "From the poster that turned Bob Dylan into an icon to the logo that helped revive a flagging city, he gave sharp outlines to the spirit of an age."[33]

The Bronx-born Glaser, who died in 2020, created the promotional poster for singer Bob Dylan's 1967 *Greatest Hits* album. The illustration features a simple silhouette of Dylan's profile with his unruly hair morphing into psychedelic wildness. "The poster is a stunning example of how Glaser could untangle a complicated concept with a simple, bold graphic," Gopnik explains. "It marks the transitional moment, captured in the album, when Dylan's virtuous folk sermons . . . ripened into his visionary imagistic anthems. . . . The poster is not simply of the time. It *describes* the time, in graphic detail."[34]

Like Rockwell, Glaser's influence was felt over several decades. And in 1977 Glaser created another iconic image—the stacked "I 'heart' NY" logo. The logo was commissioned by the state of New York (but adopted by New York City) to transform the state's crime-ridden image into one that beckoned as an international tourist destination. Glaser reportedly scribbled the logo on the back of an envelope with a red crayon in a taxi on his way to the meeting with representatives from the state government, but that simple sketch turned into a statement of identity and pride for millions of New Yorkers and has become a must-have souvenir for visitors to the city.

The envelope resides in New York's Museum of Modern Art. It is considered one of the most successful advertising campaigns in history, generating over $30 million dollars a year—and that is not counting products sporting the logo illegally.

JR: The Power of Paper and Glue

French photographer JR works with paper and glue. He enlarges black-and-white portraits and pastes them around communities—something he has done anonymously since the mid-2000s. JR's art highlights people who often go unseen by mainstream society. For one project, he created an enormous photo of a group of inmates from California's Tehachapi prison. The inmates, along with a few guards, pasted the photo in strips onto the prison's yard. Prisoners from different gangs and backgrounds—many serving life sentences—chatted about "little things" such as the project or weather, throughout the day. JR explains to NPR:

> But those little things actually reveal the humanity of each other. . . . That chitchat right there is a game changer, because when that project's over, everything goes back to normal. Well, those guards will never see those inmates the same way, and the inmates will never see those guards the same way. And what happened—which I could never believe it in a lifetime—they've asked the guards to vouch for them if they would go to board parole again. And it's incredible to think that just a piece of paper and a community action can have such an impact.

Quoted in Manoush Zomorodi, "How Paper and Glue Rekindled a Sense of Hope in a Supermax Prison," NPR, March 31, 2023. www.npr.org.

"That little scrap of paper is probably worth as much as a small Picasso," Glaser told the *Telegraph* in 2011. "In the beginning, it wasn't even copyrighted, because for the first ten years the idea was to let everyone use it, so that it would proliferate and enter into the culture."[35]

And Glaser was not done. In 2014 he created a memorable promotional image for AMC's *Mad Men*. Brilliant in its execution, it harkened back to both the Dylan poster and the slick ad men of 1960s Madison Avenue, a type Glaser knew well. A stark black-and-white silhouette of the show's lead character, Don Draper, is shown from behind, sitting, one arm casually draped across the arm of the chair, cigarette dangling from his hand while watching an array of brightly colored psychedelic images. At eighty-five, Glaser was still making people talk.

Banksy: The Unknown Influencer

Banksy, a contemporary graphic artist based in the United Kingdom, makes people talk as well, but not just about his art—despite being perhaps the most successful street artist of all time. Political activist Banksy (a pseudonym) first came to notice in the early 1990s as a graffiti artist. Although some believe him to be from Bristol, England, his identity has yet to be confirmed.

Banksy started out like most street artists by using spray paint. But at eighteen, while he was painting with some friends, the police showed up, making him question his method. Will Ellsworth-Jones shares Banksy's own words in a 2013 *Smithsonian* magazine article: "I spent over an hour hidden under a dumper truck with engine oil leaking all over me. As I lay there listening to the cops on the tracks, I realized I had to cut my painting time in half or give it up altogether. I was staring straight up at the stenciled plate on the bottom of the fuel tank when I realized I could just copy that style and make each letter three feet high." Banksy also saw stenciling as a political statement. "All graffiti is low-level dissent, but stencils have an extra history. They've been used to start revolutions and to stop wars."[36]

WORDS IN CONTEXT

antiauthoritarian/antiestablishment art: Art that critiques the unquestioned following of governments, law enforcement bodies, or social traditions

Stencils gave Banksy's antiauthoritarian art a distinctive look, one he could repeat at will. *Girl with Balloon* is one example. Originally a 2022 street mural, his most popular work features a little girl reaching toward a red, heart-shaped balloon that is floating away. In 2018 Banksy re-created the image on canvas and enclosed it in an ornate frame; the artwork sold at Sotheby's London (an art auction house) for $1.4 million. Moments after the final bid, a hidden shredder in the frame sliced two-thirds of the canvas before stopping.

Alex Branczik of Sotheby's said this was "the first artwork in history to have been created live during an auction."[37] It was widely speculated that Banksy's stunt was a commentary on art and capitalism, a recurring theme in his work, and he subsequently released a YouTube video showing him installing the shredder and activating it remotely. However, he noted that during testing the mechanism did not jam, meaning he intended the image to be destroyed completely.

Banksy also uses his art against political injustice and war. To protest the building of the West Bank wall between Israel and Palestine, Banksy created another much-repeated image, *Love Is in the Air*. Also known as *Flower Thrower*, the mural features a masked militant tossing flowers instead of a rock. During 2003 to 2015, Banksy produced over a dozen more murals in the area to support Palestine and to highlight the Syrian refugee crisis. And in 2022 Banksy completed a series of murals amid the rubble of Ukraine to protest the Russian invasion.

Shepard Fairey: Make Art Not War

Graphic artist and activist Shepard Fairey is not that different from Banksy. Although he does not work anonymously, the American-born Fairey started out as an antiestablishment street artist and uses his art primarily as political commentary. Fairey is a poster and mural artist from Charleston, South Carolina. Through the use of provocative slogans and bold colors, he calls out issues such as gun violence, climate change, the abuse of power, and the excesses of capitalism. Like Banksy, Fairey uses spray paint and stencils and has been arrested more than two dozen times for vandalism. Fairey has painted over one hundred murals worldwide, many of them commissioned—including the ten-storey 2014 Nelson Mandela fresco in Johannesburg, South Africa.

Fairey first gained notoriety during his 1989 *Obey* and *Andre the Giant Has a Posse* sticker campaign. The campaign, which questioned following authority blindly, evolved into Fairey's wildly

Graphic artist and activist Shepard Fairey is known for posters and murals that feature provocative slogans and bold colors. This one appeared at an exhibit in France.

successful *Obey* clothing line, which has led some Fairey fans to reconsider his anticapitalism messaging.

Fairey's most recognizable work is the 2008 *Hope* poster of then presidential candidate Barack Obama. Digitalizing a photo of Obama that he found online, Fairey added an overlay of red, white, and blue, along with the word "Hope" along the bottom. The poster circulated as a meme on social media and was widely seen as capturing the mood of not only Obama's supporters but an era. The poster led to more fame, though some of it was unwanted.

Fairey was sued (and lost) for copyright infringement by the Associated Press, which owned the original photo of Obama.

Fairey went on to create a series of similar posters. They included celebrities such as Kobe Bryant, Michael Jordan, and Muhammad Ali—as well as non-celebrities in a trio of posters entitled *We the People* and featuring three women of different minority groups.

Fairey also did album cover designs for musicians such as the Black Eyed Peas, Led Zeppelin, and the Smashing Pumpkins. However, his collaboration with heavyweight corporations Adidas, Nike, and Pepsi has been interpreted as selling out by his fans. Fairey has countered his detractors by reminding them that he is an activist first and uses his branded graphic art to fund his graffiti art.

Causes Fairey has supported in the past include Black Lives Matter, the Women's March, gun control, voting rights, democracy, and environmental protection. And from 2018 to 2019, Fairey designed two iconic posters in red, black, and white harkening back to the 1960s antiwar protests: *Make Art Not War*—a play on the antiwar slogan "Make Love Not War"—and *Guns and Roses*, featuring three military-style guns pointed skyward with a single red rose coming out of each of their barrels.

Paula Scher: Painting with Words

No discussion of graphic artists would be complete without Paula Scher. Scher is a contemporary American graphic and environmental graphic designer who is best known for her use of typography in her work.

Scher creates images and tells stories with the shapes of letters and words. Her most well-known and iconic work is a poster design for *Bring in 'da Noise, Bring in 'da Funk*, a New York public theater production. The poster featured a dancer surrounded by blocks of bold text in multiple fonts, weights, and sizes shooting out in various directions and angles.

WORDS IN CONTEXT

environmental graphic design: Art that incorporates design elements such as graphic design, landscape, architecture, and lighting

Going to Hollywood

Many graphic artists work in the film industry. In addition to designing corporate logos, New York's Saul Bass was a renowned graphic designer who won an Oscar for his film work. Bass, who died in 1996, is best known for creating movie title credits and posters. For director Alfred Hitchcock's *North by Northwest*, Bass invented kinetic typography, moving or animated text, as a way to communicate emotion in the opening credits before the movie even starts.

Chip Kidd from Shillington, Pennsylvania, also made his mark in the film world. Kidd has worked for Knopf, a book publisher, since 1986. Although he has designed thousands of book covers, including several for DC Comics, Kidd's biggest claim to fame is his cover of Michael Crichton's *Jurassic Park*, which features a Tyrannosaurus rex skeleton. For the 1993 movie version of the best-selling book, Universal Studios and director Steven Spielberg looked at more than one hundred logo designs. None were right, so Kidd was brought on board to reimagine his original logo. Referred to as "Logosaurus" by fans, the iconic logo was also used for the movie's accompanying theme park and licensed merchandise. Over the years, the logo has been further tweaked for subsequent movies in the franchise.

Scher, who collects old fonts that she sometimes uses in her work, majored in illustration in art school. "I really didn't draw well," she explains in the online magazine Designboom, "but I learned to illustrate with type."[38] After Scher graduated in 1970, she worked in the music business. She designed hundreds of album covers for musicians such as the Rolling Stones and Michael Jackson and was nominated for multiple Grammy Awards. And as the first female partner at the world-renowned design agency Pentagram—a company she has worked for since 1991—Scher became known for some high-profile logos, such as those for Coca-Cola, Microsoft Windows 8, and CNN. Scher's iconic style includes large-scale, hand-painted maps that feature colourful fonts arranged in the shape of an area's landmarks. Her map of Munich, Germany, covered the floor of Munich's Die Neue Sammlung—The Design Museum as part of her 2023–2024 immersive art installment called *Type Is Image*, which collected examples of Scher's work from the past five decades. Renowned graphic designer Debbie Millman said, "The museum highlights [Scher's] belief that 'words have meaning, and type has

Graphic artist Paula Scher is known for her use of typography. She creates images and tells stories by manipulating fonts, words, and shapes—as in this poster she designed for a play about Elvis Presley.

spirit,'—that people recognize type and understand the emotion, wit, power, and beauty behind it without reading."[39]

Scher was initially challenged on how to present her work, which included a Porsche that she had hand-painted with typography during the COVID-19 pandemic. The museum space was two open floors with a 30-foot (9.1 m) ceiling in one area, a 12-foot (3.7 m) ceiling in another, along with three columns, two small elevators, a curved wall, and a staircase. In the end, Scher did what she does best. She reimagined her art to fit the unique space by enlarging and reducing her artwork as needed in an explosion of fonts and color. "I think this is a joyful exhibit," Scher said. "Some of it is a demonstration of the breadth of my work, some of it is about the power and beauty of typography as both a communication tool and abstract form, and most of it is really about how an exhibit design creates a special environment that enables the viewer to discover what the meaning of it [is] for themselves."[40]

Seeing the World in Different Ways

Graphic artists create art as an expression of who they are. They are each unique—not only in how they express their art and share it with the world but also in what they have to say. And it is clear that these graphic artists have expressed themselves and their beliefs about both art and life. And although not all graphic artists would choose to communicate a message as overt as one of Banksy's stenciled on a wall in a war zone, many hope that their art has helped make people see the world in a different way.

Source Notes

Introduction: Worth a Thousand Words

1. Gargi Singh, "The Evolution of Graphic Design over the Past Decade," LinkedIn, March 3, 2023. www.linkedin.com.

Chapter One: The Evolution of Graphic Art

2. Hestie Barnard Gerber, "Ten Oldest Known Cave Paintings in the World," The Archaeologist, December 18, 2022. www.thearchaeologist.org.
3. Norman Rockwell Museum, "The Art of Norman Rockwell." www.nrm.org.
4. US Department of Labor, "Rosie: By Any Other Name—the Riveting True Story of the Labor Icon." www.dol.gov.
5. Harold Stark, "The Years in Retrospect: How Photoshop Has Shaped the World of Graphic Design," HuffPost, September 9, 2016. www.huffpost.com.
6. Rangan Das, "The Impact of Technology on the Graphic Design Industry," Artwork Flow, October 27, 2023. www.artworkflowhq.com.
7. Mirage News, "Memes and Society: A Cultural Phenomenon in Digital Age," June 26, 2023. www.miragenews.com.
8. Samantha Spiro, "The History of Graphic Design," Linearity, May 24, 2022. www.linearity.io.
9. Erik Ofgang, "What Happens to Illustrators When Robots Can Draw Robots?," *New York Times*, November 4, 2023. www.nytimes.com.
10. Quoted in Ofgang, "What Happens to Illustrators When Robots Can Draw Robots?"
11. Lucy Marino, "2024 Salary and Employment Trends Creatives Should Know," *Graphic Design USA*, 2024. https://gdusa.com.
12. Das, "The Impact of Technology on the Graphic Design Industry."

Chapter Two: Visual Storytelling

13. Magipik, "The Art of Storytelling Through Visual Design," Medium, December 10, 2023. https://medium.com.
14. Vinnie Wong, "What Is Visual Storytelling? How to Engage and Inspire Audiences," Piktochart, October 17, 2023. https://piktochart.com.

15. Wong, "What Is Visual Storytelling?"
16. Peggy Carouthers, "Printmaking Techniques You Should Know," *Art & Object*, December 22, 2022. www.artandobject.com.
17. Monica Galvan, "The History of Graphic Design," Flux Academy. www.flux-academy.com.
18. Quoted in Art Story, "Shepard Fairey: American Street Artist, Graphic Designer, Illustrator and Activist." www.theartstory.org.
19. Quoted in Will Ellsworth-Jones, "The Story Behind Banksy," *Smithsonian*, February 2013. www.smithsonianmag.com.
20. Wong, "What Is Visual Storytelling?"

Chapter Three: Graphic Design and the Art of Selling

21. Upwork Team, "Illustration vs. Graphic Design: Key Traits and Differences," Upwork, September 16, 2022. www.upwork.com.
22. Nataliya Kosmyna, "Attending to Visual Stimuli Versus Performing Visual Imagery as a Control Strategy for EEG-Based Brain-Computer Interfaces," National Library of Medicine, September 5, 2018. www.ncbi.nlm.nih.gov.
23. Because of Marketing, "How Coca Cola's Branding and Storytelling Defines Christmas," December 11, 2023. https://becauseofmarketing.com.
24. *Adobe Express* (blog), "14 Print and Digital Advertising Examples to Inspire Your Next Brand Campaign," Adobe, December 5, 2023. www.adobe.com.
25. Quoted in Kelsie Rimmer, "Art, Advocacy & Developing Creative Agency with World-Renowned Designer Jessica Walsh," Envato Elements, January 18, 2024. https://elements.envato.com.
26. Andrew Warner, "The Art and Science of Logo Design," Maverick, February 10, 2023. www.maverick-intl.com.
27. Quoted in Warner, "The Art and Science of Logo Design."
28. Magipik, "Understanding the Impact of Typography in Design Is Crucial," Medium, July 7, 2023. https://medium.com.
29. Quoted in TED, "Design and Discovery," 2003. www.ted.com.

Chapter Four: Legendary Graphic Artists

30. Cerebral Currents, "Art as a Reflection of Society: Understanding the Cultural Impact," Medium, August 2, 2023. https://cerebralcurrents.medium.com.

31. Norman Rockwell Museum, "The Art of Norman Rockwell."
32. Norman Rockwell Museum, "The Art of Norman Rockwell."
33. Adam Gopnik, "How Milton Glaser Made America Cool Again," *New Yorker*,
34. Gopnik, "How Milton Glaser Made America Cool Again."
35. Quoted in Alastair Sooke, "Milton Glaser: His Heart Was in the Right Place," *The Telegraph* (London), February 7, 2011. www.telegraph.co.uk.
36. Quoted in Ellsworth-Jones, "The Story Behind Banksy."
37. Quoted in CBS News, "Banksy Reveals How Painting Was Supposed to Fully Self-Destruct," October 18, 2018. www.cbsnews.com.
38. Quoted in Andy Butler, "Paula Scher Interview," Designboom, July 10, 2013. www.designboom.com.
39. Debbie Millman, "For Paula Scher, Type Is Image," *Print*, July 21, 2023. www.printmag.com.
40. Millman, "For Paula Scher, Type Is Image."

For Further Research

Books

Tammy Gagne, *Become a Graphic Designer*. San Diego, CA: BrightPoint, 2021.

Steven Heller et al., *Milton Glaser: POP*. New York: Monacelli, 2023.

W.L. Kitts, *The Art of Graphic Communication*. San Diego, CA: ReferencePoint, 2020.

Don Nardo, *Exploring Careers in the Creative Arts*. San Diego, CA: ReferencePoint, 2024.

Paula Scher et al., *Paula Scher—Type Is Image*. Cologne: Walther König, 2023.

Internet Sources

BanksyFilm, *Shredding the Girl and Balloon—the Director's Half Cut*, YouTube, October 17, 2018. www.youtube.com/watch?v=vxkwRNIZgdY.

BC Productions, *The Shocking KFC Chicken Shortage: What Happened?*, YouTube, November 3, 2022. www.youtube.com/watch?v=ZULMrEGZZcM.

Bradshaw Foundation, "Cave of Lascaux: Cave Paintings of Southwestern France." www.bradshawfoundation.com.

JR, "Tehachapi, The Yard: California USA, 2019," JR personal website. www.jr-art.net.

Lucy Marino, "2024 Salary and Employment Trends Creatives Should Know," *Graphic Design USA*, 2024. https://gdusa.com.

Debbie Millman, "For Paula Scher, Type Is Image," *Print*, July 21, 2023. www.printmag.com.

Amrish Mudgal, "What Is Graphic Design? A Beginner's Guide (2023)," Pixpa, February 27, 2023. www.pixpa.com.

Websites

AIGA
www.aiga.org
Founded in 1914 and formerly known as the American Institute of Graphic Artists, AIGA is a professional association for American designers. The organization's website features articles, design resources, professional development opportunities, a career guide, and a job board.

Die Neue Sammlung—The Design Museum
https://dnstdm.de
The website for Die Neue Sammlung—The Design Museum—includes information and images of graphic artist Paula Scher's immersive *Type Is Image* exhibition, which features a retrospective of Scher's work from the past five decades.

Graphic Artists Guild
https://graphicartistsguild.org
The Graphic Artists Guild is an American organization for graphic and interactive designers, illustrators, animators, and web programmers and developers. Its website offers resources, webinars, and articles of interest to graphic artists. The guild also provides a database of artists and acts as an advocate for its members and industry.

Graphic Design USA
https://gdusa.com
Graphic Design USA is a business resource for graphic design professionals based in the United States. It offers a print and online magazine, a monthly newsletter, career tips, and an annual list of up-and-coming designers.

Society of Illustrators
https://societyillustrators.org
The Society of Illustrators is dedicated to the promotion of the art of illustration. The nonprofit, established in 1981, offers opportunities to exhibit, educational programs, juried competitions, and lectures.

Index

Picture Credits

Cover: Denel/Shutterstock

6: Newscom
9: Prisma/Newscom
13: Tester128/Shutterstock
15: Patti McConville/Alamy Stock Photo
21: RGG Media/Shutterstock
24: Stocktrek Images, Inc./Alamy Stock Photo
30: Randy Duchaine/Alamy Stock Photo
34: Janet Julie Vanatko/Shutterstock
36: adsR/Alamy Stock Photo
41: Herbert Ortega/Alamy Stock Vector
46: Randy Duchaine/Alamy Stock Photo
51: Associated Press
54: Paula Scher/La Nacion de Costa Rica/Newscom

About the Author

W.L. Kitts is a professional freelance writer and children's book author who is based in Canada.